*For my mother—Wietse Fossey*

First published in the United States, Great Britain, Canada, Australia, and New Zealand in 2012 by North-South Books Inc.,
an imprint of NordSüd Verlag AG, CH-8005 Zürich, Switzerland.
Translated by David Henry Wilson.
Distributed in the United States by North-South Books Inc., New York 10017.

Library of Congress Cataloging-in-Publication Data is available.
ISBN: 978-0-7358-4079-9 (trade edition)
Printed in China by Leo Paper Products Ltd., Heshan, Guangdong, October 2011.
1 3 5 7 9 · 10 8 6 4 2

www.northsouth.com

FSC
www.fsc.org
MIX
Paper from
responsible sources
FSC® C020056

# The
# Clever Little Witch

*By Lieve Baeten*
*Illustrated by Wietse Fossey*

NorthSouth
New York / London

The sun went down, and the moon came up. It was the time when all good witches rise and shine. "Come on, Cat!" cried the Little Witch. "Let's do a bit of math. One wee-wee plus another wee-wee make . . . Soon you'll be a big, clever cat. One sandwich plus another sandwich . . ."

*CLUNK! PLUNK!* "What was that?"

A suitcase! There was a little suitcase standing outside the door. Curious, the Little
Witch shook the suitcase from side to side. "Maybe there's a magic potion in it, or a new
witch's hat. Come on, Cat," said the Little Witch, "I'll magic the suitcase open."

"Hocus-pocus, witch's ride,

Little suitcase, open wide!"

"What's happening?" The coffeepot, the cactus flower, the cake tin, and everything else around Lizzy flew open. But not the little suitcase—it was still firmly closed.

"Come on, Cat," said Lizzy, "let's go and find someone to help us!"
Suddenly, high up in the night sky, she saw a witch with a suitcase.

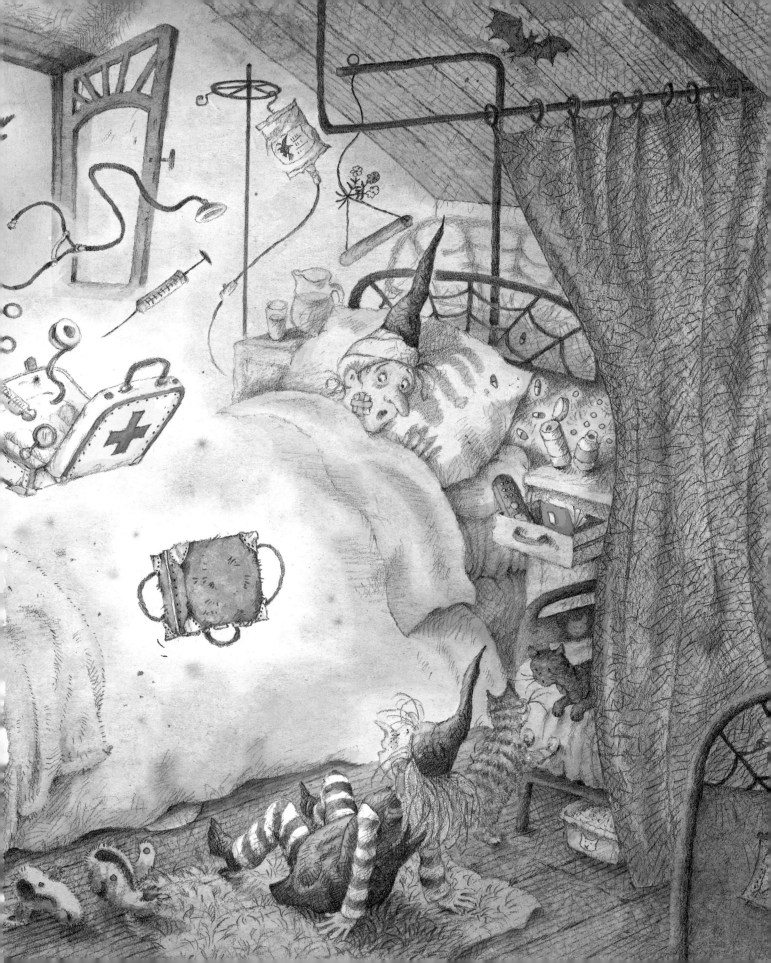

The witch was flying straight toward the Witch Hospital. Maybe she's ill.
Curious, Lizzy and the cat flew after her.

It was all quiet and peaceful in the hospital.

"Hello, Lizzy," said the Witch Doctor. "What are you doing here? Are you ill?"

"No!" said Lizzy. "I'm not ill. I just want to know what's inside this suitcase."

"Don't you know the magic spell?" asked the Witch Doctor.

"Yes," said Lizzy, "but it doesn't work. Watch!

"Hocus-pocus, witch's ride,
Little suitcase, open wide!"

The box of pills, the doctor's case, the hospital windows, and everything else around Lizzy flew open. But not the little suitcase—it was still firmly closed.

"I think that's the little suitcase for big witches," said the doctor. "Take good care of it until you're big and clever enough."

"All right," Lizzy said to herself. "I'll go and find someone else who can open the little suitcase."

High up in the night sky she saw another witch with a suitcase. Maybe this witch would
be able to help her. Was she about to go on a journey? She was actually heading straight for
the Witch Train Station.

The Witch Train Station was very crowded and very noisy.

"Hello, Lizzy," said the Traveling Witch. "I see you've got a suitcase. Are you going on a journey?"

"No!" said Lizzy. "I'm not going on a journey. I just want to know what's inside this suitcase."

"Don't you know the magic spell?" asked the Traveling Witch. "The one that enables you to open things?"

"Yes!" said Lizzy, "but it doesn't work. Watch!

"Hocus-pocus, witch's ride,
Little suitcase, open wide!"

The blue suitcase, the green suitcase, and everything else around Lizzy flew open.
But not the little suitcase—it was still firmly closed.

"Ah well, Lizzy," said the Traveling Witch, "it's probably the little suitcase for big witches.
Take good care of it until you're big and clever enough."

Now Lizzy couldn't see anyone else who could help her.

"Come on, Cat," she said, "let's fly home and do a bit more math."

But Lizzy couldn't get the mysterious suitcase out of her mind. She thought and thought, and thought again.

At last she said out loud: "When I say the magic opening spell, the suitcase doesn't open but stays firmly closed. . . . So what would happen if I wished for it to stay closed?"

"Once more. I shall try it just once more."
The cat kept as still as a mouse. Lizzy cried:

"Hocus-pocus, witch's flight,
Little suitcase, stay shut tight!"

Everything around Lizzy remained shut tight. But not the little suitcase—it was now wide-open. "You see, it worked," the Little Witch said happily. "I did it!"
In the little suitcase there was a letter. Lizzy read the letter out loud:

Lizzy would have liked to know who had written the letter. Quickly she packed everything into the little suitcase, and she flew as fast as the wind until she came to the hill with three trees. And then, suddenly, she saw where she was going: she was flying straight toward the Witch School.

"Hello, Lizzy," said the Witch Teacher. "What are you doing here? I wasn't expecting to see you."

"Well, I found this little suitcase, and I magicked it open," said Lizzy. "And here I am."

"But that's the little suitcase for big witches," said the Witch Teacher. "And you got it open all by yourself? Then you really are big and clever. Welcome to the Witch School."

"Of course I'm big and clever," thought Lizzy. "That's what I've always been."

*Lieve Baeten* (1954–2001) was born in Zonhoven, Belgium. She studied illustration at the Academy for Fine Arts in Antwerp, and it was always her dream to publish a picture book of her own. The dream came true in 1992 with the publication of *The Curious Little Witch*. It was not long before the adventures of Lizzy were translated into many languages and awarded many prizes, and took their magic all around the world.

*Wietse Fossey*, who was born in 1977 in Antwerp, Belgium, is Lieve Baeten's son. He studied graphic design at the Karel de Grote College in Antwerp and today creates Internet sites and flash animations in the field of multimedia.

When Lieve Baeten died in a car accident in 2001, the text of *The Clever Little Witch* was already written, and there were some sketches as well as some finished pictures. From the existing material and with the aid of computer graphics, Wietse Fossey was able to complete the book.

It was his wish that *The Clever Little Witch* should reach the hands of the children for whom it was intended.